Calvin Coconut

DOG HEAVEN

CALViN CoCoNut

DOG
HEAVEN

Graham Salisbury

illustrated by
Jacqueline Rogers

A yearling Book

Text copyright © 2010 by Graham Salisbury
Illustrations copyright © 2010 by Jacqueline Rogers

All rights reserved. Published in the United States by Yearling, an imprint of Random House Children's Books, a division of Random House, Inc., New York. Originally published in hardcover in the United States by Wendy Lamb Books, an imprint of Random House Children's Books, a division of Random House, Inc., New York, in 2010.

Yearling and the jumping horse design are registered trademarks of Random House, Inc.

Visit us on the Web! www.randomhouse.com/kids

Educators and librarians, for a variety of teaching tools, visit us at www.randomhouse.com/teachers

The Library of Congress has cataloged the hardcover edition of this work as follows:
Salisbury, Graham.
Calvin Coconut : dog heaven / Graham Salisbury ; illustrated by Jacqueline Rogers.
p. cm.
Summary: When his teacher asks him to write a persuasive argument about something he really wants, fourth-grader Calvin creates a unique way to express his desire for a dog.
ISBN 978-0-385-73703-6 (hc) — ISBN 978-0-385-90641-8 (lib. bdg.) — ISBN 978-0-375-89541-8 (ebook) [1. Dogs–Fiction. 2. Composition (Language arts)–Fiction. 3. Schools–Fiction. 4. Family life–Hawaii–Fiction. 5. Kailua (Oahu, Hawaii)–Fiction.] I. Rogers, Jacqueline, ill. II. Title.
PZ7.S15225Cac 2010
[Fic]–dc22
2008049871

ISBN 978-0-375-84602-1 (pbk.)

Printed in the United States of America
10 9 8 7 6 5
First Yearling Edition

For Pato
In memory of Jackie

Dogs make the world a nicer place
—G.S.

For Angela with love
—J.R.

1

Manly Stanley

Everyone in class held their breath as Mr. Purdy dangled a squirming cock-a-roach over the brand-new resort he'd made for Manly Stanley.

Manly Stanley was our class pet, a centipede.

A *large* centipede.

Rubin could hardly stand it. "Drop it, Mr. Purdy, drop it."

Manly Stanley's new home sat on Mr. Purdy's desk. It was an old, cleaned-up fish aquarium. Inside, a big craggy rock and a branch of twisty driftwood sat on a beach of white sand. There was even a marooned pirate ship for Manly to explore.

I could see him looking at me through a cannon port. "Calvin, my man," he seemed to say. "S'up?"

I'd captured Manly Stanley in my bedroom and brought him to school, and now look at him. What a setup.

"Centipedes are predators," Mr. Purdy said, looking down at Manly Stanley. "They use their claws to capture and paralyze their prey."

Yow! I hoped that cock-a-roach could run fast.

But it was hard to imagine Manly Stanley as a predator. I mean, all he did was hang out. He slept. He looked at you. He scurried into the pirate ship when he wanted some privacy.

The crowd squeezed in around Mr. Purdy.

"Move," someone said. "Let me see!"

"Look how Manly's checking out that bug."

"How come you're putting that poor little cock-a-roach in there, Mr. Purdy?" Shayla asked.

"Breakfast."

Shayla's mouth fell open. "Eew, sick!"

"It's what centipedes eat, Shayla. Spiders, too, and earthworms."

"Yuck."

Julio scoffed. "Not yuck, Snoop. *Yum.* You don't remember when you ate that worm?"

I spurted out a laugh. Julio called her Snoop right to her face. But Snoop fit, because she was nosy. And the story about her eating the worm was true, but she only ate the head. Back in kindergarten, some kid brought a soup can full of compost worms for show-and-tell. At lunch, he stuck one into her tuna sandwich when she wasn't looking. Shayla chomped it down. All us guys thought we were going to die from laughing so hard.

Shayla squinted razor-slits at Julio.

Mr. Purdy dropped the roach.

It must have sensed danger, because it sprang toward the rock. "Dang," Rubin whispered. "Look at him run."

"Okay," Mr. Purdy said. "Back to your seats. Time to get to work. Nothing's going to happen to that roach anytime soon."

"Aw, man," Julio said. "I want to see Manly eat it."

Mr. Purdy clapped his hands. "Let's go! Chop-chop!"

I plopped down at my seat in the first row by the window. Manly

Stanley's resort was right in front of me.

I looked out the window, remembering a pet I once had, sort of. A dog named Chewy, a beagle who liked to shred rubber slippers. But Chewy was really my dad's dog, and when my dad moved to Las Vegas to be a famous singer, Chewy went with him.

At least now I sort of had Manly Stanley as a pet. But he couldn't shake hands like Chewy, or run down a tennis ball, or snore in my room at night.

Sometimes I really missed Chewy.

And my dad.

2

Boing!

Once we were back in our seats, Mr. Purdy rubbed his hands together. "Okay, boot campers, listen up."

Mr. Purdy had been in the army, which is how we came to be called boot campers. We liked it.

"This will be fun," he went on. "Because

today we're going to do some writing!" He raised his fist. "Woo-oo!"

Everyone groaned.

Rubin wailed from the back row. "No, Mr. Purdy, noooo!"

Mr. Purdy smiled. "Oh yes, Mr. Tomioka. And more importantly, we'll be *re*writing to make what you write better."

I covered my ears. Writing was a brain twister. Rewriting was a brain *exploder*. First you had to make something out of nothing. Then you had to make that something better. "It's too hard, Mr. Purdy!"

"Exactly, Calvin! That's why we do it. No pain, no gain."

We all groaned and made like we were dying until Mr. Purdy hissed like a snake. "Sssssssss."

"Sssssssss," everyone hissed back.

That's how he got us to be quiet.

I grinned at Willy, down at the other end of the front row. Willy grinned back.

Mr. Purdy raised a finger. "One page. That's all I ask. You can do that in your sleep. First draft is due on Friday. But here's the best part: We're going to get started right now!"

Shayla, who sat next to me, waved her hand. "What are we going to write about?"

"Excellent question, Shayla. Thank you."

Shayla glanced around like, Look, everyone, I'm smart.

Mr. Purdy grabbed a felt marker. "Here's your topic."

On the whiteboard he scribbled: *What I Want So Badly I Can Taste It.*

"I want a bike!"

"I want a guitar!"

"I want recess!"

"I want—"

Mr. Purdy raised his hands. "Hang on, boot campers, there's more. In one page I want you to tell me what you want and why you want it.

But here's the deal: I want you to *persuade* me—your reader—that you should have it. I want you to *sell* me your idea."

I perked up. Sell? That part was good.

Kai raised his hand. "My dad sells kayaks."

Then Jolena. "My dad sells houses."

Rubin jumped in with "My dad sells insurance."

"*Moms* sell stuff, too," Doreen said. "Not just *dads*."

Rubin snorted. "They boss you around and make you do stuff."

I looked back at him. "Hey, Rubin. You forgot my mom sells jewelry at Macy's?"

"Oh ... yeah. Calvin's mom sells stuff. But not yours," he said to Doreen. "She just picks you up from school."

"During her break, you crippled ant. She's a dental assistant."

Mr. Purdy paced in front of the class. "So listen

9

up. Here's how it works. Persuasive writing is like writing an advertisement, or an article in a newspaper that tries to get you to do something, like recycle or volunteer."

I looked at Manly Stanley. He was creeping toward the rock. I leaned closer.

"Someone here wanted a guitar," Mr. Purdy said. "Was that you, Calvin?"

"Uh . . . what?"

"I thought so, and you know what, Calvin? I love guitars, too. But that *you* should have one might be hard to sell to me, your teacher, because if you had a guitar you might spend all your time playing it and never do your homework. See the problem?"

"Uh . . ."

"Good. So, how are you going to convince me that you should have a guitar? That's your challenge. See? And remember, I'm a tough customer."

The classroom fell silent.

"Wow," Mr. Purdy said. "I can hear all of

you thinking about what you want so badly
you can taste it."

I looked out the window at the blue sky.

What *do* I want?

I turned and saw Manly Stanley, now almost
to the rock. I knew what *he* wanted, and I bet he
could almost taste it, too.

What do I want that bad?

Boing! An idea! "Yes!" I whispered.

3

Like Chewy

After school, I headed over to the first-grade rooms to get my sister, Darci. I spotted Tito Andrade, the sixth-grade pocket-change thief, making some poor third grader empty his pockets. His friend Frankie Diamond was watching. I slipped around the corner. I'd been robbed before.

I poked my head into Darci's classroom.

"Well, hello, Calvin Coconut."

"Ms. Wing . . . is Darci here?"

"She's just cleaning up."

Darci was at the sink with a handful of wet paper towels.

"Hi, Calvin."

"We gotta go home."

Darci jammed the wad of paper towels down into the wastebasket. "Bye, Ms. Wing."

"Thanks for helping me, Darci."

Willy, Julio, Rubin, and Maya were waiting for us out on the grassy field behind the school. In the distance I was relieved to see Tito Andrade and Frankie Diamond walking home ahead of us . . . not that I had anything in my pockets worth taking. Tito was such a bully.

We headed home.

Maya shook her head. "I still don't know what I'm going to write for Mr. Purdy."

"Me either," Julio added. "How about you, Calvin?"

"Still thinking." I had an idea, but it had a big problem.

"Do you have to write something, Calvin?" Darci asked.

"Yeah, we all do."

"About what?"

"Something we want so bad we can taste it."

"Like food, you mean?"

"Could be anything. Like a skateboard, or a bike, like that."

Darci frowned. "But if you taste it, it has to be food, right?"

"No. You can taste other things."

"That's just weird, Calvin."

I shrugged.

"I know what I'm writing about," Willy said. "Cuttlefish."

Julio and I stopped. *"Cuttlefish?"*

"No, really," Willy said. "I just want to *like* it, that's all . . . like you guys do. Like everybody around here does. I feel weird being the only one who doesn't. The problem is, cuttlefish is

disgusting. It stinks. It looks like long stringy boogers. What is it, anyway?"

"It's sort of half octopus, half squid."

Willy shook his head. "Totally gross."

I put my arm around his shoulder. "I got some bad news for you. You ready?"

"Shoot."

"You. Are. Strange."

"Forget cuttlefish," Rubin said. "I want a snake."

Julio scoffed. "Good luck with that. Snakes are illegal here, and anyway there aren't any snakes in Hawaii."

"Oh yes there are," Maya said.

Rubin's face lit up. "Really?"

"Yup. Blind snakes. They eat ants and termites."

"How you know that?"

"National Geographic."

Rubin rubbed his chin. "Do they bite?"

Maya grinned. "Yeah, but only Japanese boys, like you."

"Really?"

I laughed. "That was a *joke,* Rubin. Jeese."

We walked on.

I thought: So what if my idea has a problem? It's what I want, isn't it? "A dog," I said. "That's what I want. A dog."

"But you can't have a dog," Darci said. "Stella's allergic."

And that was the problem. "To cats, Darce, not dogs."

Stella lived with us and helped Mom. She was sixteen. Because she was allergic to cats, Mom thought she should stay away from dogs, too, just in case.

"But you're only writing about it," Willy said. "You're not actually *getting* it."

"Yeah, just writing."

When Darci and I got home we found
Mom's boyfriend, Ledward, in
our driveway. He was hunched
over our half-dead lawn
mower. It was idling, and
gray smoke billowed
around him. The noise
was as loud as a truck
dumping gravel.

The lawn mower
gagged, spat, and died
as we walked up.

Ledward stood and shook
his head. "Grass too long." He

glanced toward our front yard, which sloped down to the river.

I shrugged. It was too long weeks ago.

Ledward was always telling me I should help Mom out more and mow the lawn, too. But pushing a lawn mower through grass that thick was like trying to ride your bike in soft sand. I hated that job.

Darci went into the house.

Ledward and I stood looking at the grass. The river was rusty brown. My red skiff lay in the swamp grass above the waterline.

"You want me to help you cut it, boy?"

Time to change the subject. "Did you ever have a dog when you were a kid, Ledward?"

4

If I Had a Dirty Dog

"Well, now," Ledward said.

He squatted on his heels and crossed his arms over his knees. I squatted, too, both of us facing the river.

"I had about seven dogs, at various times. No, eight. Counting one that ran away."

He chuckled. "That one wanted to be his

own boss. These days I have four. But hunting dogs, ah? Not pets."

"There's a difference?"

"Sure. Hunting dogs you train to track pigs. They're scrappy." He winked at me. "Not good house dogs. Too nervous."

"I want a dog."

Ledward nodded. "Every boy should have a dog."

"Mom won't let me. Stella's allergic to cats, and maybe dogs. Her eyes get all puffy."

Ledward rubbed his chin. "Well . . . maybe you could keep it in the backyard. Or in your room, keep it out of the house."

That could work. My room was made of half the garage. It wasn't really part of the house. Hey, I should put all this in my essay.

"I'm supposed

to write about it for school. I mean, how I want a dog. Mr. Purdy says I have to sell it to him . . . the idea, not a dog."

Ledward shook his head and smiled. "Daniel . . . to you, he's Mr. Purdy . . . anyways, he had dogs as a kid, too. He had this one white one that loved mud. Hoo, that was one dirty mutt. All the time, he had to hose him off, all the time."

Ledward and Mr. Purdy had grown up together. They were friends then and were still friends now.

I lifted my chin toward the river. "If I had a

dirty dog, he could just jump in the water and wash off."

"Sure."

Ledward went back to the lawn mower and pulled the cord. Coughs and spits. He tried again. Still nothing.

"Shoot," he mumbled. He adjusted the choke and tried again. The lawn mower shook, rattled, and went back to sleep. "You don't use this enough."

"Yeah, but can you think of a way I can persuade Mr. Purdy that I should have a dog?"

Ledward pushed the lawn mower into the garage. "Just bring up dogs, and boom! You got him. But if you want a for-real dog, it's not Daniel you need to sell. It's your mama. That might be tougher than Daniel."

"Impossible, you mean."

"If you can't get a dog, how's about a parakeet? Or maybe some fish?"

"I like birds and fish, but they don't care about you. Know what I mean? Dogs do."

Ledward put his hand on my shoulder, bent down, and whispered, "I got something to show you." He looked toward the house. "She home, the girl?"

He meant Stella. Ledward always called her *the girl.* Stella's job was to go to school, and to help Mom, who worked on the other side of the island. Stella's favorite thing to do was make my life miserable.

"I hope not."

"Go check. Leave her a note if she's not. So she won't worry. Tell her I taking you for a ride. I bring you back before supper. Get Darci. We take her, too."

"Where?"

"Surprise."

5

Maunawili

Stella wasn't home yet. Darci was lying on the floor watching cartoons. "Ledward wants to take us somewhere."

"Where?" she said, not looking away from the TV.

"He said it's a secret." I started to write the note.

Darci hit the remote. "Let's go!"

Ledward started the jeep. I sat in front, and Darci had the whole backseat to herself.

Ledward waited. "Click it or ticket." We buckled up.

Since the jeep was built before seat belts, Ledward had made some out of army surplus straps. They weren't pretty, but they did the job.

He drove slowly, taking his time. Hawaiian style.

The old army-green jeep had a friendly growl to it. The breeze swirled in and the heat of the engine warmed my feet. "I like your jeep."

Ledward looked over at me. "Not many of these still around anymore. Just a few heaps covered by weeds, too far gone to fix. Rust eats the steel."

"You fixed this one, right?"

Ledward nodded. "Me and my pops. We cleaned it up, kept it in a garage out of the rain."

"You have a dad?"

Ledward laughed, loud and long. "And a mama, too, by golly. What? You thought I came from a store?"

"What I meant was, I never knew you had a dad. That's all. I mean, you never said . . . you . . ."

That was dumb, I thought, sliding down in my seat.

"S'all right, boy, s'all right." Ledward tapped my knee. "I only joking with you."

We drove out of Kailua town and headed inland toward the mountains. I'd known Ledward for almost a year, but really, what did I know about him? Not much.

"Where we going?"

He looked over and winked.

We turned onto a smaller road and headed into a jungle, green and thick.

Darci's eyes were big as mangoes. "Where are we, Ledward?"

26

"Maunawili."

On and on we drove, snaking up the twisty old road. Dirt driveways crept off into the jungle like overgrown paths. If they led to houses, I sure couldn't tell. But I did see the flash of a silver roof.

Trees branched over the road, blocking the sun. It felt like we were driving into the throat of a whale.

"Almost there," Ledward said.

He waved to an old man hacking weeds with a machete. It was the first person we'd seen since we left the highway. The man lifted his chin as we drove by.

"Where is it, exactly, that we're going?"

"My place . . . I going show you my pet."

"A dog?"

Ledward shook his head. "Better."

6

The Banana Grove

Ledward turned into a banana grove, a thick leafy forest of green. The air grew sweeter.

"Wow," Darci whispered, gawking up at the fat banana tree leaves.

Ledward lifted a hand off the steering wheel. "This is where I grew up. My pops, Uncle Shorty, bought this farm way back in early times. He lives in Kaneohe, now, in a condo. But back then he grew bananas, papaya, avocado, mint."

"How come you call your dad Uncle Shorty?"

Ledward chuckled. "His friends called him Shorty in high school. The name stuck. And all my friends called him uncle. So, Uncle Shorty. He's retired now."

That confused me. Ledward was as tall as a telephone pole. "Your dad's short?"

"Six foot six."

Wow.

"I took this place on when my parents moved," he continued. "Long time, my family been here. Now it's just me, my dogs, and my pig. I don't have any sisters or brothers."

"Dogs?"

"You see."

How come Mom had never said a word about his place? She must have known about it. "Has Mom been up here?"

"Sure. In fact, she got a little garden."

"She does?"

"I show you."

I frowned. "She never told us."

The jeep bounced and jerked along ruts in the road. The old seats squeaked. The engine growled low.

After a moment, Ledward said, "Your mama is cautious."

"What do you mean?"

"Well . . . I'm sort of like the new kid on the block. Takes a while to get to know the new kid, ah?"

The dirt lane burst out of the bananas into the sun. Ledward's house sat in the middle of a large, neat grassy yard. The house was dark red with white around the edges. It had a silvery tin roof and stood off the ground on legs, with white slats around the base.

"Wow. Nice place."

Ledward pulled up on the grass and shut the engine down. A gray dove landed on the hood of the jeep.

Ledward whistled softly and the dove flew off.

So quiet.

"Where are the dogs?"

Ledward lifted his chin. "Out back."

"They don't bark?"

Ledward winked. "They know my jeep."

"Cool."

I saw them in my mind. Hunting dogs. Long fangs and fur that stuck up on their backs. Danger in their eyes.

Ledward got out of the jeep. Darci stood, and he lifted her up and sat her on his shoulders, holding her feet. We headed around to the back of the house.

Ledward pointed his chin toward a patch of dirt. "That's your mama's garden."

Why hadn't Mom told us she'd been here?

"The pig is still young," Ledward said. "I call him Blackie."

"You named a pig?"

"Sure. He's a good pig. There's my dogs."

Four dogs looked out at us, each in its own

wood kennel with a wire door. Like the house, the kennels stood off the ground on stilt legs.

The dogs paced behind their wire doors. One of them growled, its head low.

"Hush," Ledward whispered.

The dog whined. It was dirty white with black spots. It didn't have fangs or hair standing up on its back. It was a scruffy dog—skinny, even. All of them were.

Ledward pointed to each of them. "Typhoon, Paco, Snake-eye, and Jimmy."

"Man oh man," I whispered. Hunting dogs. If only my friends could see this.

Darci wrinkled her nose. "Something stinks."

Ledward chuckled. "That would be Blackie."

7

Blackie

Like Manly Stanley, Ledward's pig had his own resort—a slimy, stinky, mud-sucky pigpen.

Blackie wasn't as fat as the pigs I'd seen in books at school. He wasn't pink, either. He had short black hair and was as scrappy as Ledward's dogs.

Darci crouched and looked through the wire fence. "He looks like he's smiling."

"He's a happy pig."

Lazy, too. He was lying on a pile of hay under a slant-roof shelter, smiling and winking flies away.

Ledward snapped his fingers. "Hoo-ie." He made kissy sounds, like when you call a dog.

Blackie lumbered up and waddled over. He stuck his flat nose through the wire and snorted.

Darci jumped back.

The sound was deep. I reached over the fence and scratched the stiff hair behind Blackie's ear. Dried mud flaked off.

Ledward reached over to scratch him, too. "Good boy, Blackie." Just like you'd say to a dog.

I looked up at Ledward. "A pig is a nice pet, I guess. But it can't do what a dog can do, like follow you on your bike, or catch a Frisbee or tennis ball. A pig . . . well, it just . . . stinks."

"You think? Watch this."

Ledward opened the gate and snapped his fingers. Blackie waddled out and followed him around to the front yard.

Darci and I looked at each other. "Weird," she whispered.

"No kidding."

The caged dogs eyed everything that moved as we hurried to catch up with Ledward. "Where are we going?"

"For a ride."

"In the jeep?"

"Yup."

Ledward snapped his fingers and pointed to the front passenger seat. Blackie waddled up and tried to jump in. But he was too fat. He couldn't even get a foot up.

Ledward bent down and put his arms under him. "When he was small, I just scooped him up and dropped him on the seat. He's a big guy now." Ledward grunted as he hefted the pig onto the seat.

Blackie sat, smiling.

That is one strange pig, I thought.

Ledward scratched at a block of caked mud on Blackie's back and brushed away the dirt. "Hop in," he said.

Darci and I climbed over the back tire into the jeep.

Soon we were driving back through Kailua with Blackie sitting up front like somebody's German shepherd, nose high, sniffing the air.

People in cars and on the sidewalks gaped, pointed, and laughed their heads off.

Ledward smiled and waved.

Julio, Willy, Rubin, and Maya would never believe this. Calvin, they'd say. Pigs don't ride in jeeps.

I looked at Darci. "You think Mom would let me get a pig for a pet, Darce?"

8

Dander Bugs

That night I took my spiral notebook and a chewed-up pencil and climbed the ladder to my bunk. The faint smell of gas from the lawn mower crept in under the door. Or maybe it was from Mom's car, which was only a few feet away on the other side of the wall.

I lay on my stomach, thinking.

Outside, inches from my face, small moths fluttered against the window screen. The light in my room drew them out of the night like a magnet.

I tapped the pencil against my teeth. What should I write about, a dog or a pig? Stella wasn't allergic to pigs, so maybe—

Bam!

I jumped and the pencil flew from my hand.

Bam! Bam!

Jeese! *"What?"*

"Open up!" Stella yelled.

"Why?"

"I have something for you."

Bam! Bam! Bam!

"All right, all right, I'm coming."

I slid off the bunk.

When I opened the door, Stella shot me.

"Hey!"

Stella aimed the orange squirt gun at my face and fired again.

"What'd you do that for?"

"That's for getting into my Diet Sprite, twerp. Next time, ask."

"I didn't get into your dumb Sprite."

"That's *Diet* Sprite, and you stole my empties."

Well, she was right about that. I'd taken them to Kalapawai Market and turned them in for money to buy *her* a birthday present. "How was I supposed to know you wanted them?"

Stella shot me again. "Guilty as charged."

I backed away, trying to block the water with my hands.

Stella kept shooting. I was soaked. "I'm telling Mom, Stella. You're in trouble."

"Go ahead. Tell. It's worth it."

I ducked and dodged while Stella squirted me until the gun ran out of water. I wiped my face. "I'll get you for this."

Stella blew me a kiss. "Looking forward to it, sweetie."

I slammed the door and locked it, then moved my desk chair over and propped it under the doorknob. "Wart face," I muttered.

I changed my T-shirt and climbed back onto my bed.

What I wanted so bad I could taste was suddenly clear. I picked up my pencil and wrote:

What I want so bad I can taste it is for Stella to get a big fat wart on the end of her big fat nose. My wish should come true because she's an ugly toad and ugly toads have warts, lots and lots of warts. And since it's totally unfair to get squirted because of some dumb pop cans, Mr. Purdy should want my wish to come true. Because he's a fair teacher. And boot campers should stick together. Against all enemies. Forever and ever.

Yeah!

Maybe it wasn't what I was supposed to write, but it felt good. I grinned. Then I tore the paper out of my notebook and tossed it toward the wastebasket.

Missed.

I ran the pencil under my nose. It smelled good. What I wanted was a dog. But I couldn't get one. So what was I going to write?

Argh!

This assignment was hard.

Hey . . . I banged my forehead with the palm of my hand. Duh . . . this isn't for real. I can write whatever I want.

I want a dog!

I erased the exclamation point. Too much.

I want a dog, because I love dogs . . .
except I probably don't want a hunting
dog. Dogs like people. Cats mostly don't,
except for Maya's cat, Zippy. Zippy is
cool. But dogs are better.

It was a start. Not a very good one, but I could make it better later. What next?

I want a dog that can keep up with my bike.

I erased it.

I want a dog that likes to run.

Erased that, too.

I grinned, thinking how awesome it would be to have a dog next time Stella banged on my door. It would bark and spit out the dander stuff that makes her eyes puff up and she'd scream and run for her life. Ho, yeah! How funny would *that* be?

New ideas popped up like popcorn.

I could train it to follow Stella around like a shadow. I could make a sign for my door: BEWARE! DANDER BUGS!

I could—

I put my pencil down and rolled over

onto my back. The black spider on the ceiling above my head was still in its same spot. It hadn't moved in a week. Maybe it ate a fly and wasn't hungry. I squinted at it. Was it even alive?

I put my hands behind my head.

How do you get something you can't have?

9

Don't Be Shy-la

Mr. Purdy was excited.

And that made us all nervous.

He rubbed his hands together. "It's Friday, boot campers. First-draft day!" He raised his fist as if this was the greatest thing since Batman tangled with the Joker. "Who's going to read first?"

I put my head down and shielded my eyes with my hand, whispering, "Not me, not me, not me."

"Nobody?"

That classroom got so quiet I looked up to see if everyone was still there. Manly Stanley was watching me from the resort on Mr. Purdy's desk. Was that fool grinning?

"Oh, come on, guys," Mr. Purdy said. "Where's your confidence?"

Even Shayla kept quiet. So quiet that I thought I heard Manly Stanley burp. Where was that roach, anyway?

"Shayla?" Mr. Purdy said.

Shayla's paper was lying upside down on her desk. She touched it but didn't turn it over. "It's not very good yet, Mr. Purdy."

Mr. Purdy snapped his fingers. "Exactly, Shayla. That's part of what I'm trying to teach you. Your first draft isn't meant to be a great work of art. But you know what? You can make it better. Trust me, all of you, no matter how bad you think your first draft is, you can fix it. So, let's hear what you've written, Shayla."

Shayla turned her paper over and started reading.

"I want—"

She stopped. "Everyone will laugh."

Mr. Purdy went over to the list of class rules and tapped number six: *Never laugh at someone else's mistakes*. "First of all, whatever you've written is not a mistake. And even if it were, it would not be laughed at, would it, class?"

"No, Mr. Purdy," everyone mumbled.

"Go ahead, Shayla."

"Don't be shy-la," Rubin whispered, loud.

I looked back and grinned.

Mr. Purdy gave Rubin his *cork it* squint.

Shayla read, "I want to take yoga lessons."

She waited for everyone to laugh.

I thought, Yoga? What's yoga?

Shayla read more.

"I want to take yoga lessons with my mom,

because she says they make her feel young and healthy. Mr. Purdy should want me to take yoga lessons, too, because I would do it with my mom. And I would get better grades, because I would be young and healthy like my mom."

Mr. Purdy smiled. "Very good, Shayla. Thank you. Yoga is an excellent practice, and doing something with your mom would be wonderful. Good work. Who's next?"

I slid lower in my seat.

Mr. Purdy brightened. "Rubin. Great. Let's hear it."

Rubin stood and cleared his throat.

"I want a skateboard because skateboards are cool and if I had one I could race Maya and beat her because I'm a boy. Mr. Purdy will want me to have a skateboard because he's a boy, too."

Maya looked at Rubin like, That has GOT to be the STUPIDEST thing I have ever heard in my LIFE!

I covered my head and laughed. If that was a page of writing, his letters had to be six inches tall.

"You're right, Rubin," Mr. Purdy said. "I am a boy. But you're dreaming if you think you can beat Maya on a skateboard."

Maya smiled at Rubin.

"That's a good start, Rubin. Thank you for trying. Who's next?"

Willy was erasing something on his paper. Maybe he'd wanted a skateboard, too.

Mr. Purdy looked my way. "Mr. Coconut, what have you got for me today?"

Dang.

10

Pretzels

My paper was in my pocket. I'd folded it down to the size of a postage stamp. I took it out, unfolded it, and looked up.

Mr. Purdy nodded.

"I want . . . a dog . . . maybe a small one, but not too small. I don't want something that yaps and looks like a rat."

Mr. Purdy laughed, and when everyone saw he thought it was funny, they laughed, too.

I went on, feeling braver. "Mr. Purdy should want me to have a dog because it will make me get better grades."

Now the class really laughed. Julio whooped in the back.

Mr. Purdy held up his hands for quiet. "Just how might a dog make you do that, Calvin?"

"Well, see . . . if I have a dog I'll be happier, and if I'm happier I'll work harder, and if I work harder, I'll get better grades. Get it?"

Mr. Purdy nodded. "If that's all it takes to get better grades, I'm bringing everyone a dog tomorrow."

Rubin started barking. The whole class joined in.

"Ssssssss," Mr. Purdy hissed.

"Ssssssss," everyone hissed back.

"I like your thinking, Calvin. And you grabbed my attention. We'll talk about going deeper after we hear a few more essays, so hang on to your good thoughts."

"I can do that."

But which thoughts were the good ones?

After a few others read their papers, Mr. Purdy said, "Good work, all of you. You make me proud. Now it's time to talk about revision."

"Aww, man."

"It's too much work."

"It's junk."

Mr. Purdy sat on his desk next to Manly Stanley's resort. Manly was trying to climb the glass.

I grinned. Maybe Manly wrote a paper, too, and he was trying to get out so he could read it: *What I want so bad I can taste it is another big fat juicy cock-a-roach!*

"This weekend," Mr. Purdy said, "take what you've written and make it better. Especially your opening sentence. That sentence has to pick me up and shake me. You understand what I'm saying?"

Not really.

"For example," Mr. Purdy went on. "Instead of Shayla saying she wants to take yoga lessons, she could open with something like this: *If you've ever seen someone twisted up like a pretzel, you know that yoga is an amazing practice.* See? Now we're interested, because a person twisted up like a pretzel is unusual. We try to imagine it."

Shayla nodded.

Mr. Purdy spread his hands. "Now, I know yoga isn't about pretzels, but that word does create an interesting image. That's what I want you to do with your opening sentences. Make them more interesting. Invent your own pretzels."

A pretzel?

Boy, was I stumped.

11

Streak

After school, Darci, Julio, Willy, Rubin, and I kicked across the grassy field, heading home.

I was thinking.

Sometimes Mr. Purdy was strange. Invent your own pretzel?

But it did get my attention.

Okay. So I could write: *A dog is like a pretzel.*

Dumb. No way is a dog like a pretzel. Then I thought, Hey! Ledward's pig!

A pig in a jeep would be a monster pretzel. I mean, who could resist wanting to hear more about *that*? So maybe Ledward's pig was my pretzel.

But if I'm writing about a dog, how can I make a pig my pretzel?

I kicked a crushed pop can on the side of the road. It skittered past Darci and Julio, who were walking in front of me.

Julio looked back. "How come you so quiet?"

"I'm thinking."

"About what?"

"Pretzels."

Julio grunted.

Okay, I thought, how about this: *A dog is like a pig in a jeep, only he's riding with a kid on a bike. The dog's name is . . .*

What is his name? I liked Streak.

Streak.

Yeah.

Ho! The *second* I named that dog, he be-came real. Alive. Streak was a real dog. He was living somewhere right now. Or was Streak a girl dog? He or she was probably a puppy curled up in a cardboard box in some-body's laundry room.

Streak.

Once I had that name, ideas came down like rain in the mountains. Let's just say he's a boy dog.

His name is Streak and his ears are flapping in the wind.

Yeah, yeah, yeah!

I had to get home and write this stuff down before I forgot it. I grabbed Darci's hand. "We got to run!"

Julio called after me. "What's the hurry?"

"I just thought of my pretzel!"

12

Two Birds with One Crumb

I sat at my desk and scribbled down everything I could remember. I read it out loud to see how it sounded. I fixed a few things and read it out loud again. Not too bad. My opening sentence would pick Mr. Purdy up and shake him!

Another thought started to itch. Ideas are

like that, fuzzy at first; you sort of feel them. Then they grow, and if you're lucky, they pop your eyes open.

Hmmm.

If I do this right, I might be able to feed two birds with one crumb. I could get a good grade *and* . . . ho, yeah! . . . I could use my essay on Mom! To get a dog! For real!

This is genius!

That evening after dinner I hung around the kitchen. Mom and Stella were washing dishes.

"Here," I said, handing Stella my plastic juice glass left over from breakfast. It had dried-up orange juice on the bottom.

Stella squinted and grabbed the glass.

Mom smiled. "Thank you for helping, Cal."

"That's what I'm here for."

Stella rolled her eyes. "Spare me."

Mom set the glass in the

soapy sink. "Did you get a letter from your mom today, Stella?"

"No." It was almost a whisper.

Mom paused. "That's too bad."

And it was too bad. Stella hadn't gotten anything from her mom in weeks, not even a birthday card. Stella had just turned sixteen.

Mom handed a plate to Stella to dry. "You know how slow the mail can be between Texas and the islands."

Stella scoffed. "Yeah, the Pony Express has a problem with oceans."

"Oh, Stella."

"It's okay. I don't mind."

Mom nodded. "Your hair looks lovely today, Stella. You should wear it up more often."

Stella shrugged.

I looked for more stuff to help with. My cereal bowl was right where I'd left it that morning before school. A fly floated in the evaporating milk at the bottom. I took the fly, wrapped it in a napkin to give to Manly Stanley on Monday, and stuffed it in my pocket.

I handed the bowl to Mom.

"Thank you, Calvin. I like it when you help out."

I smiled.

Stella tossed the dishtowel over her shoulder and squinted at me. "He's not helping out. He wants something."

Mom raised an eyebrow. "Is that right, Cal?"

"No, really, I'm just helping out. You know, cleaning and stuff."

Stella smirked.

"Great," Mom said. "Please take out the trash."

Stella winked.

I hated taking out the trash and she knew it. The garbage can in the garage smelled worse than a bloated maggoty dead toad. "Sure, Mom."

I reached under the sink and pulled the packed bag out of the trash can.

Stella shook her head. "Don't you see it, Angela? He doesn't want to help out. He wants something. I know he does."

"I do not!"

"Just take out the trash, Calvin," Mom said.

I took it out and dumped it, holding my breath. Who

cared if Stella ever got a letter from her mom? Not me!

I stumbled back into the kitchen, gasping for air.

"Mom, can I read you something I wrote? It's for school."

"Homework?"

"Yeah, homework. I worked on it all afternoon."

"Really?"

"Well, sure, Mom."

Mom dried her hands. "I'd love to hear it, Calvin."

I pulled a folded piece of paper out of my pocket.

Stella leaned against the counter and crossed her arms. "This I have to hear."

DOgS StiNk

"Close your eyes . . . I mean, you know, to see it better."

Mom closed her eyes.

Stella stuck her finger in her nose.

I ignored her and started reading.

"A dog is like a pig in a jeep, only he's riding on a bike with a kid. His name is Streak and his ears are flapping in the wind. He's a puppy and needs a home and—"

"Hah!" Stella yelped. "There it is. He wants a dog!"

The next spider I found was going between her sheets! And I knew just where to find one.

Mom opened an eye. "Is this some new way you've invented to ask me about getting a dog?"

"No, Mom, this is a for-real assignment for Mr. Purdy."

Mom raised an eyebrow.

"Really," I said feebly. My plan had just blown up.

"You *know* we can't have a dog, Cal. Stella might be allergic to them like she is to cats. It's the dander. Besides that, dogs stink."

"Willy's dog doesn't stink . . . too much."

"Well, anyway, you've seen how Stella's eyes puff up. She can hardly see."

Stella stuck her pointy head into the matter. "I'm pretty sure I'm not allergic to dogs, but still, they carry ticks, fleas, lice, and diseases. Their tongues are cities of disgusting bacteria."

"They are not! They–"

The phone rang.

Stella grabbed it. "Hello?"

She frowned and handed me the phone.

I took it. "Hello?"

It was Ledward. "I just thought of something. You know the lawn mower?"

"Yeah."

"Maybe it was out of gas. Run into the garage and check it for me. I'll wait."

"Be right back."

I set the receiver down. "Gotta check some-thing for Ledward."

When I came back, I told him, "It has gas."

"Shoot. Well, it was just a thought."

"Ledward?"

"Yeah?"

I stretched the cord as far away from Mom and Stella as it would go. I squatted down and whis-pered into the phone, "Can you help me with something? It's for . . . uh, school."

"How come you whispering?"

"I don't want anyone to hear."

"Got it. What's it about?"

I looked over my shoul-der. Mom and Stella were finishing up with the dishes. I turned back. "A dog."

"Ahhh, the dog again." Ledward paused. "Okay, we need a plan."

I turned when a foot with red toe-nails appeared next to me. I waved her away, but Stella just stood there.

"Saturday," Ledward said. "My day off. I come get you. We go see some dogs."

"Really?"

"Keep it to yourself."

I squished lower and whispered. "See them where?"

"Dog heaven."

14

Donkeys

On Saturday morning, I was out in the street with Willy and Julio slapping a dried-out run-over toad around with a plastic hockey stick when Ledward's jeep pulled up.

He grinned. "Toad hockey, huh?"

Julio lifted the hockey stick. "Want to play?"

"Can't. Me and Calvin got someplace to go."

"Where?"

"Place I call heaven."

Julio and Willy looked at me. I nodded.

Ledward hooked a thumb over his shoulder. "It's in town."

Julio's face brightened. "Can we come, too?"

"Sure. Go ask your parents. Be gone couple hours."

Julio and Willy ran off.

Ledward chuckled. "Your mama home, boy?"

"She had to go to work. Someone didn't show up. They needed help."

Ledward shook his head. "Too bad. She could use some time off. You and me, we got to help her more."

I nodded.

Ledward slapped the passenger seat. "Hop in."

We drove down to my house. Ledward parked and went into the garage. He rolled the lawn mower out. "Let's give this beast another try."

He adjusted the choke and pulled the cord.

The lawn mower coughed but didn't start.

"Pretty soon the grass going be too long to cut . . . with this thing, anyways. We might need a tractor!"

Ledward tried again. The lawn mower hacked like a dog with a chicken bone stuck in its throat. "Guess I should take the engine apart, clean it out."

Sounded good to me.

"When we get back I take um home."

Darci came out. "Ledward!"

Ledward rubbed her head with his big hand. "Darci girl, you want to come see dog heaven?"

"What's dog heaven?"

Ledward gave her a light shove toward the house. "I show you. Go tell the girl you and Calvin going someplace with me."

"But she's still asleep."

"Okay." Ledward put his hand on my shoulder. "You go write a note. Tell her I took both of you someplace so she won't worry."

What a laugh. Stella wouldn't worry about me if I was halfway down a shark's throat. But she would worry about Darci.

I ran into the kitchen and scribbled a note: *Me and Darci went with Ledward.* I signed it: *Calvin Coconut.*

I ran back out and hopped in the jeep.

We headed down the street, grabbing Julio and Willy on the way.

Darci sat in front. I squeezed onto the back-seat with Julio and Willy.

Ledward hummed and tapped the steering wheel with his thumbs. "You kids going like this place."

I jiggled my leg and grinned into the wind.

Dog Heaven

Ledward pulled into a parking lot in front of a low building shaded by three huge monkey-pod trees. We jumped out.

"Yah!" I yelped.

The parking lot was sizzling hot, even though the bottoms of my feet were as tough as cardboard. I leaped over to the grass. Darci got a ride on Ledward's shoulders.

I read the sign. HUMANE SOCIETY.

Inside, the first thing that hit me was the smell. "Ho, stink, this place."

Ledward laughed and pointed. "Look."

Cats. All in what looked like a giant playhouse with lots of windows. People were crammed inside playing with them. Ledward set Darci down and she ran over to join them.

"We going be by the dogs," Ledward called. "Come find us when you done."

"I will." Darci didn't even look back.

The dogs were in concrete kennels with chain-link dog runs. Most kennels held only one dog, but some had two. The dogs seemed happy, wagging their tails, barking. Some were stretched out and didn't get up every time somebody poked a hand through the fence. The pit bulls looked scary. Would anyone ever take them home?

Julio was amazed. "So many dogs!"

Willy elbowed me. "Are you getting a dog?"

I shrugged. "Not really."

"Well, if you could, which one would it be?"

I frowned. How would you even choose?

Ledward squatted down next to me. "Watch um. See how they act. Are they friendly, nervous, bark a lot? Pretty soon you get a feel. A couple will stick in your head. Those ones, you look closer."

Julio, Willy, and I studied every dog in the shelter. Most of them were kind of strange, with long bodies and big heads. Some of them wouldn't stop barking. Those, I'd never be able to take home. But they'd be good watchdogs.

Ledward followed us, not saying much.

I couldn't choose. But some I liked.

"Was me," Ledward said, "I know which one I would take."

"Which one?"

He shook his head. "You first. Which one do you keep coming back to?"

"Well . . . there's one. But it looks kind of mean."

"I don't think they'd let people take them home if they were mean."

"Its eyes are weird."

"Show me."

I headed back a few kennels and crouched. "That one."

Willy, Julio, and Ledward crowded over me.

It was a small dog. Black, with a white chest and a black nose. It sat looking at us.

"Hmmm," Ledward said. "I see what you mean. Those eyes look like they seen some things. He's wary, checking us out. But I don't think he's mean."

The dog studied us, silent and alert.

"Streak?" I said. "Is that you?"

The dog's ears perked up.

"Ho," Ledward said. "Look how he reacted."

"Streak," I said again. "Come here, boy."

The dog got up and trotted over.

"Look at that," Julio whispered.

Willy crowded closer. "He's friendlier than he looks."

Slowly, I stuck my fingers through the fence.

The dog nosed closer. He sniffed my fingers. "Hey, boy. Yeah, you're a good dog."

He leaned up against the fence. I looked at Ledward, who nodded. I turned back and stroked the dog with two fingers. He was warm. His eyes closed.

"It's you, isn't it? You're Streak."

And that did it.

The dog sprang up and ran in circles around the cage, stopping to look every time he passed me. Around and around. No barking. Just energy.

Julio laughed. "Man, first he's a lump and now he's a rocket."

Ledward put a hand on my shoulder. "I think he likes you."

After about five million trips around the cage, the dog came back and leaned against the fence again. He panted, his wet tongue jiggling.

Ledward stood and read the ID card on the cage. "Ooops. This dog is female. Her name is Ruby. Border collie mix. A year old."

"She sure is fast," I said.

"Does it say why she's in here?" Julio asked.

Ledward checked the card again. "Stray, is all it says. Probably ran off or got lost. Who knows?"

Willy shook his head. "Nice dog, spooky eyes."

Ledward crossed his arms. "One thing for sure. She's a herding dog, and herding dogs need lots of exercise."

"If she was mine," I said, "I'd take her

everywhere I went. She could sleep in my room, too. Stella wouldn't be allergic if she was out there, right? Can I get her, Ledward?"

"Whoa, slow down, boy. You want to get me in trouble with your mama?"

Ledward grinned and leaned close. "But if it was up to me . . . I take um out right now. Boom!"

I stood.

"But." Ledward raised a finger. "It's not up to me."

The spooky-eyed dog looked up at me.

Zero, I thought. That was what my chances were.

Ledward put his hand on my shoulder. "I like one of the pit bulls, but that's your dog, boy. No question. That's your dog."

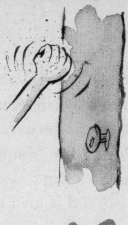

16

Frankie "Dog-Lover" Diamond

That night I couldn't sleep.

I couldn't sleep the next night, either.

Like a jackhammer, worry rattled in every corner of my brain. What was Streak doing? Was she wondering where I went? Or worse, had someone adopted her and taken her home?

Stop!

Monday morning when my alarm went off, I was so tired I fell back asleep.

Bam! Bam! Bam! Pounding on my door. "Get up! You're late!"

Stella.

"I'm up, I'm up."

"If I have to come out here again, I'm coming in."

I dragged myself out of bed and got dressed in the same stuff I'd worn the day before. I was awake enough to remember to shake my clothes out first. Once, I put my pants on with a centipede in them. Yah! I could still feel it crawling down my leg.

I stumbled into the kitchen. Mom was making lunches. Stella was nibbling on a carrot and checking her homework.

Mom put the back of her hand on my forehead. "You okay, Cal?"

"I didn't sleep much."

"Something bothering you?"

"No . . . Yes . . . Not really."

Mom studied me.

Stella snorted without looking up.

Mom went back to making lunches. "If you want to talk about it, I'm here."

I poured myself a glass of orange juice.

Stella looked up. "Angela, look! Your son used a glass!"

I stared at the orange juice without drinking it.

"All right, Calvin," Mom said. "Spit it out. What's bothering you?" She crossed her arms and waited.

"Can I get a dog?"

Mom sighed and yanked the dishtowel off her shoulder. "We've been over this before, Calvin."

"I know, but I found—"

"We can't have one around the house. The answer is still no. No, no, no."

Stella snapped off a bite of carrot.

Later that day after I got home from school, and after I waited for Stella so she could watch Darci, I jumped on my bike and headed for the Humane Society. I had to know if Streak was still there.

"Calvin!"

I looked up and saw Maya sitting on her skateboard in her driveway. She pushed herself toward the street with her hands. "Where you going?"

"See a dog."

"What dog?"

"My dog."

She eyed me. "You don't have a dog."

"So?"

"Can I come with you to see the dog you don't have?"

I nodded. "Get your bike. It's not close."

We rode side by side, saying little. I was glad I didn't have to explain everything to Maya. She was good that way. If you wanted to be weird, fine. If you wanted to keep a secret, no problem.

We slowed and stopped when we saw a guy weaving toward us on a bike with small wheels and tall handlebars. I bent forward and squinted. "Is that who I think it is?"

Maya nodded. "Uh-huh. Got anything in your pockets?"

"Nothing . . . but Frankie Diamond doesn't rob us like his dumb friend Tito."

"You hope."

Frankie Diamond was two years older than we were, and much bigger. It was weird to see him on a bike.

Frankie skidded to a stop. He flicked his eyebrows. "Little punks, howzit?"

Maya studied his silvery handlebars. "I didn't know you had a bike."

Frankie shrugged. "Who doesn't have a bike?"

"Tito."

"Sure he does."

"Really?"

"He just doesn't ride it."

This was interesting, but I didn't have time for it. "We have to go now."

"Where?"

"Uh . . . a place."

"We're going to see his dog," Maya said.

"Your dog don't live at your house?"

"Uh," I said. "Not yet."

Frankie looked down the street. Like he was checking to see if anyone he knew was around. "I like dogs."

I stared at him. "Uh . . . you can come, too."

Frankie turned his bike around. "Let's go."

Wow. Julio, Willy, and Rubin would never believe this.

"It's kind of far," I said.

"Pshh. Far is Tahiti. Far is Hong Kong. Where we going?"

"Dog heaven."

Frankie grinned. "Cool."

Dumped

The Humane Society wasn't crowded. It was a weekday afternoon, so people were still at work.

Streak was stretched out in her kennel.

"Yes!"

All my worries evaporated. I ran up and fell to my knees. "Streak, it's me! Come here, girl."

Streak's head popped up. Her eyes looked like bullets.

"It's me, Streak. Calvin."

Streak trotted over, her tail wagging.

Frankie looked at the ID card. "This ain't Streak, it's Ruby."

"Yeah, but I call her Streak."

Frankie knelt between me and Maya. He stuck his fingers through the fencing. Streak licked them. Frankie grinned. "Yeah, you a good dog."

Streak glanced at me and ran a circle in her cage.

Frankie laughed. "So, Coconut, if this is your dog, when you going bail her out?"

Good question. "Soon."

"You need money, or what?"

"Worse."

Streak came back and leaned up against the fence. Frankie cooed and scratched her head. "Maybe we can go inside the cage."

"You think so?"

"Never know till you ask, ah?"

Maya watched him leave. "He's not so bad. I mean . . . well . . . you know."

I nodded. It was strange, all right. Frankie's future-criminal friend Tito would never get caught hanging around a couple of fourth graders. "Funny how somebody looks mean and he's not."

"Yeah."

Frankie came back with a guy named Ben.

Ben seemed like a nice guy. He opened Streak's kennel. "I'll bring the dog to one of our acquaintance areas so you can get to know her."

"We can do that?"

"Sure you can."

Ben put a leash on Streak and took her out to a fenced area big enough for all of us. "Find me when you're done and I'll take her back."

Frankie Diamond flicked him a cool shaka, not flashy, not like a tourist. "Thanks, brah."

"No problem. You kids have fun."

Streak was as excited as a mongoose in a garbage dump. I bet she'd been cooped up for weeks. Every time someone tried to catch her, she dodged and ran faster.

Frankie shook his head. "Hoo, this mutt is a rocket."

"That's why I call her Streak."

"So, Coconut. Tell me the truth. This ain't really your dog, right? You just want her to be. Is that what's going on here?"

I nodded. "My mom won't even listen."

Frankie lunged toward Streak as she came zipping around, and Streak dodged him. "I had a dog once."

"What happened to it?"

"Got sick."

"Oh . . . sorry."

"Yeah."

We played with Streak for almost an hour before we called Ben.

"You want to take her home?" Ben asked.

I picked Streak up and hugged her. She licked my face. "How much does it cost to get a dog here?"

"Around sixty dollars."

"Sixty *dollars*?"

Ben pinched his chin in thought. "Well . . . look at it this way. Sixty dollars is a good deal. If someone gave you a dog for free, you'd still have to take it to a vet for tests and vaccinations. Right? Then you have to get a dog tag and all that. Could cost you closer to five hundred. But this dog comes with all of that already done. So sixty dollars is not a bad deal."

I didn't even have sixty cents. And Mom sure wouldn't give it to me.

Ben reached out and ran his hand over Streak's head. "A policeman found her in the mountains last week."

Frankie frowned. "Somebody dumped her?"

"That's likely." Ben shook his head. "How people can do that, I don't know. They could have found her a home, nice dog like this."

We all looked at Streak.

Ben elbowed me. "Look how she stares at you."

"This kid calls her Streak," Frankie Diamond said.

Ben chuckled. "Maybe we should change the name on the card."

"Write that she's taken, too," I added.

"You want her?"

"Yes."

"Bring your parents in. But come soon. I don't think she'll be here long. Not this dog."

18

Boys Stick Together

Two days later. Sun going down.

It was around six o'clock and I was alone in my room. Mom wasn't home from work yet and Darci had gone to Kalapawai Market with Stella.

I stared at my essay. Mr. Purdy's one-page assignment had somehow grown four legs and a beating heart. My imaginary dog had become real. Her name was Streak, and I wanted to rescue her.

So much I could taste it.

Outside an engine rumbled.

I peeked out the window as Ledward pulled up and parked on the grass. He lifted our lawn mower out and rolled it into the garage, then went back to his jeep.

I went out to him.

"Hey," he said. "S'up?"

"Not much."

He tossed me a small bag of charcoal.

"What's this for?"

He flicked his eyebrows. "Steaks."

He took a covered bowl off the backseat. Inside, five steaks swam in a rich brown marinade. It smelled so sweet it made my stomach gurgle.

"All right!"

Ledward smiled. We went into the house.

He set the bowl on the counter. "Got that lawn mower fixed. Gas line was clogged."

"Oh. Good. I guess."

Ledward dipped his head toward the back-yard. "You know how for start the hibachi?"

"Sure."

"Good. Get um good and hot. I make rice."

The hibachi was a small black grill that sat on the ground. To cook on it you had to squat like a toad.

Just as I was about to head out to the patio, Stella and Darci walked in. When Stella saw Ledward she frowned. "Where's Angela?"

"Not home yet," Ledward said, ignoring Stella's gloomy face. He was lucky he could do that. Her frowns always made me want to be some-where else.

Ledward rinsed the rice, poured it into the rice cooker, and added water. "I'm cooking to-night. Teriyaki."

Darci's eyes lit up. "Can I help? Can I, can I?"

"How's about you make a salad?"

I went out and got the charcoal going. If Streak was here, I'd give her some of my steak. Man, would she love that!

What if some mean family had taken her home? Tied her up with a rope or put a shock collar on her?

Then I felt guilty, because that wasn't a very nice thing to think. Mean families don't rescue dogs. They dump them in the mountains.

There was a commotion in the kitchen. Mom was home.

A minute later she came out with a glass of lemonade and dragged a plastic patio chair over. She kissed the top of my head and sat. "How's my little man of the house?"

"Good."

"I'm so glad I'm not cooking tonight. This is so nice of Ledward."

I nodded.

She closed her eyes and took a deep breath.

I looked at her. Poor Mom. She had a long day.

Ledward brought the steaks out and squatted next to me. "Coals look good. Let's do it."

Ledward let me put the steaks on the grill. They sizzled, and I breathed in the sweet aroma.

Ledward dragged a chair over and sat next to Mom.

She tapped his knee. "Thanks for the surprise dinner."

"No problem."

They sat in silence.

I smiled. If Streak was here she'd be sitting next to me with her eyes pinned on those steaks.

We ate out on the patio. Somebody's dog barked.

Ledward grinned. "When I was a boy in Kaneohe, I had this crazy dog. That mutt ate anything—socks, towels, string, toilet paper, whatever." He sighed. "Best dog I ever had. He went everywhere with me."

I looked up from my plate.

Ledward winked.

I glanced at Mom, who was cutting a piece of steak.

Ledward went on. "You know . . . the way I see it, every boy needs a dog sometime in his life."

Mom put her knife and fork down and looked at him. "You boys sure do stick together, don't you?"

I glanced at Stella. Her face was blank.

Ledward chuckled, pretending he hadn't heard Mom. "Me? I had seven dogs."

Mom rolled her eyes. "Stella's allergic to cats, Ledward. And maybe dogs, too. How many times do you boys have to hear it? Besides, if we had a dog, who'd end up caring for it? We all know the answer."

I jumped in. "No, Mom. I'll take care of it, I promise."

"Like you take care of your room?"

"Uh . . ."

"The steak was good," Stella said, then took her plate into the kitchen.

"Thank you," Ledward said.

We sat listening to the toads croaking in the swamp grass down by the canal. I stared at my half-eaten steak. My messy room had just killed any chance I'd had of rescuing Streak.

19

Got to Get Smart

Later that evening, after Mom and Ledward had come back from a walk on the golf course and I'd picked some stuff up in my room, Ledward dragged me away from the TV.

"Get the empty teriyaki bowl. Bring it to the jeep."

I took it out.

The toads were so loud now that Ledward almost had to shout. "We got to get smart, boy."

"How?"

The light from the house lit Ledward's face as he bent close. "I get my best ideas when I'm cooking on a hibachi, and tonight I got a good one."

I waited.

He glanced toward the house and whispered, "We got to take your mama to dog heaven."

I laughed. "She won't go."

"You leave that to me, boy. Your part is more important."

"What's my part?"

"Just be you." He put his hand on my shoulder and winked. "There's not a mama alive who can turn a dog away once she sees it in her kid's arms."

20

Not Me

"Write your name on a small scrap of paper," Mr. Purdy said the next day at school. "Then fold it up."

"Are we having a raffle, Mr. Purdy?"

"Is there a prize?"

"What's the prize, Mr. Purdy, what is it?"

Mr. Purdy walked down the aisles with his empty coffee cup. "Drop them in here."

"What does the winner get, Mr. Purdy?"

Mr. Purdy shook the coffee cup. "Remember your revisions? I'm drawing names to see who reads first."

"Ack!"

"Aww, man."

"Come on, Mr. Purdy."

Mr. Purdy reached into the cup. He smiled. "First up is . . . Rubin!"

Rubin groaned. I turned around and grinned.

Rubin made a big show of getting his paper out of his desk, like getting it out was a huge amount of trouble, and did Mr. Purdy really want to wait around until he found it?

"Take your time, Rubin," Mr. Purdy said. "We can wait."

Rubin's paper was all wrinkled up. He smoothed it out and cleared his throat. "Okay." He cleared his throat again. "I want a skateboard because skateboards are cool and if I had one I could race Maya and beat her because I'm a boy. Mr. Purdy will want me to have a skateboard because he's a man."

Rubin looked up, grinning.

A small laugh burst out of me like a cough.

Mr. Purdy stared at Rubin. His eyebrows were pinched like, Did I really hear what I just heard? "That's your revision, Rubin?"

"Yes, sir, Mr. Purdy."

"It sounds exactly like your first draft. What did you revise?"

"Boy."

"Boy?"

"Yeah. In my first draft I said you were a *boy.* I changed that to *man,* because if I say *man* it gives it more power, because you think if a man wants me to have a skateboard, then that means something. See?"

"Rubin?"

"Yes, Mr. Purdy . . . sir?"

"How many words are in your paragraph?"

Rubin counted. "Thirty-six."

"Before school's out I want you to rewrite your paragraph. Twenty-five words or less. Got it?"

Rubin's pained face vanished. "Only twenty-five?"

"Twenty-five."

"I can do that."

"And leave my name out of it."

"Sure . . . I mean, yes, sir, Mr. Purdy, sir."

Mr. Purdy shook his head and drew another name. "Shayla."

Shayla's revision got her a pat on the shoulder. Willy's was pretty good. Julio's got a big star, which Mr. Purdy drew on the whiteboard. Maya did okay, too.

Mr. Purdy glanced at the clock. "Time for one more."

I closed my eyes. Not me, not me, not me, not me.

"Calvin Coconut."

A-Plus, Mr. Coconut

"Uh . . . me?"

Mr. Purdy waited.

I unfolded my essay. I'd totally rewritten it, now that I knew about Streak. "Can it be a revision even if you change everything, Mr. Purdy? I mean, to make it better?"

That got me a big grin. "Bingo, Mr. Coconut, I believe you're getting the point."

"I am?"

"Look." Mr. Purdy went to the whiteboard and wrote *Revision*. "What's this word?"

"Revision."

"Correct. Now, what's this one?" Underneath it Mr. Purdy wrote *Re-Vision.*

"Revision . . . but with a line in it."

"A line?"

"Uh . . . a hyphen?"

"A hyphen. Thank you. So. When you wrote your first draft you had a *vision* of what you wanted to say. Then you thought about how to make it better, right?"

I nodded.

"You looked at it in a new way. You rethought your initial vision to make it better. Re-vision. So let's see how your revision strengthened your first draft."

For a second I panicked. Strengthened?

I started reading: "There's . . . uh, there's this small black and white dog with wild eyes and a short attention span."

Everyone laughed.

Mr. Purdy nodded to go on.

"She lives at the Humane Society. Someone drove her up to the mountains and dumped her. She's one year old and she's the fastest dog I've ever seen. I call her Streak. When I met her she was in like a cement jail cell. She came over and licked my fingers and leaned against my hand.

She was warm. I only know two things for sure. The first is, she needs a real home, because it stinks where she is."

The class thought that was hilarious.

"Go on," Mr. Purdy said, smiling.

"The second is, she . . . she needs a friend. Someone like me."

I stared at my paper.

The room was quiet.

Even Manly Stanley waited to see who would speak first.

"A-plus, Mr. Coconut," Mr. Purdy said softly. "A-plus."

22

Skeleton

Ledward might get his best ideas crouching over a hibachi, but I get mine lying on my bunk and looking out my window.

"Yes!" I whispered to no one.

I rolled over onto my back and smiled up at Spidey, still motionless in his web above my head. I was so excited I felt twitchy. My new idea was to try my A-plus revision out on Mom like before, only this time I would say it. I would make it sound like I was just talking.

I practiced all afternoon.

Mom, guess what, I saw this small black and white dog with wild eyes and a short attention span. . . .

Ho, yeah! This was going to be great!

By the time we were all sitting around the dinner table, I was as nervous as a mouse. I wished Ledward was here.

I waited for just the right moment.

Mom said, "Any mail today, Stella?"

"Just some junk mail."

"Nothing from your mom?"

"I think she might have lost her pen."

Mom reached over and covered Stella's hand with her own. "One day you'll get five letters all at once, just wait."

"I doubt that."

We ate in silence.

Do it, I thought.

I opened and closed my mouth. But all those revised words didn't want to pour out. I tried to stop my leg from bouncing.

Mom turned to me. "So, Calvin. How did your day go?"

"Well . . . uh . . ."

Stella smirked.

Just *do* it!

I leaned back, put my hands behind my head. Make it casual. Make it like you just thought of it.

Actually, I thought of something else. "My day was good, Mom. And, uh, did you see I cleaned up my room?"

"Really?"

"Yeah, and I'm going to keep it clean, too."

Mom raised her eyebrows.

I cleared my throat. "Uh, Mom? Have you ever seen Ledward's pig?"

Mom studied me a moment. "Have you?"

Ooops.

Stella spilled the beans. "Ledward took him and Darci to his house."

"Really." Mom looked at Stella, waiting for more.

Stella shrugged. "That's all I know."

"Was it wrong?" I asked. "I mean, to go there?"

"No, Calvin, it wasn't wrong. I just . . . well, I wanted a little more time to pass before you got . . . you know . . . more personal with . . . with Ledward."

"I like Ledward."

Mom smiled. "And so do I, Calvin. So. What about his pig?"

"It rides in his jeep," Darci said.

"It does?"

"In the front. With a seat belt."

Stella nearly choked on her food. "You have *got* to be kidding."

I had to get this conversation back on track. "No, it's true. Ledward's pig is just like a . . . uh . . . just like a dog I know . . . a small black and white one with . . . with wild eyes and a short attention span."

Mom studied me.

Stella threw her head back and roared.

I looked at her. What was so funny?

Her shoulders shook as she tried to stop laughing. "You're creative, I'll give you that."

I'll get you, I thought. You just wait.

Since Mom couldn't stop gawking at me, I decided to go on. "This dog—it's a girl dog, and she lives at the Humane Society, and, well, anyway, someone took her into the mountains and dumped her. She is the fastest dog I've ever seen."

Darci looked at Mom, then at Stella, then back at Mom.

I peeked over to see how I was doing.

Mom gaped at me. Maybe I was really telling it well and she was spellbound.

I felt my courage rise. "I only know two things about her, Mom. One is that she needs a home. Two is that she needs a friend . . . someone like . . . uh, someone like me."

Stella roared. "He did it again! I can see right through you! I can almost see your skeleton!"

I squinted at her.

"That's enough, Stella," Mom said.

Stella raised her hands in surrender. "Fine."

Mom shook her head and reached over to tap my hand. "That was sweet, Calvin, it really was. You're trying so hard. I didn't know you had it in you."

Did this mean I could get Streak?

Mom's eyes glistened. She patted my hand again and sat back.

Darci gave me a secret thumbs-up.

"Oh, come on," Stella said. "You don't believe he just came up with that gooey stuff, do you? Somebody wrote it for him and he memorized it. Go ahead and ask him. I bet he could say it again, word for word."

Mom laughed, dabbing her eyes with her napkin.

Stella frowned. "Think what you like, but he's a fake."

"Stella!" Mom said, then looked at me. "He's a sweetheart."

I lit up like a bug zapper. "Does that mean I can have a dog?"

Stella fake-coughed. She fake-rubbed her eyes. "Just talking about it makes my allergies act up."

The phone rang.

Darci ran to get it. She poked her head back out. "For you, Mom. It's Ledward."

Mom got up and went into the kitchen.

I shoved my string beans into a tight pile so it would look like I ate some of them. What Stella needed was a bug in her bed. Or a lizard. No, a scorpion.

"Well," Mom said, sitting back down at the table. "It looks like you have a friend, Cal."

"I do?"

"Ledward just invited me to go somewhere with him."

"Where?"

Mom put her elbow on the table and cupped her cheek with her hand. She sighed. "Does the name Streak ring a bell?"

Texas

STELLa
c/o Angela
Hawaii
USA

23

Dear Stella

It was Saturday. Stella was still asleep. Mom had already gone off to work, and Darci was watching TV.

I was just about to go down to Julio's house when I heard the mail truck.

Darci ran out and came back with an Eddie Bauer catalog, a wad of newspapery junk mail, two bills, and something for Stella that looked very much like it might be a birthday card.

There was a return address with no name.

I showed it to Darci. "Look. It's from Texas."

"Is it from her mom?"

"Got to be."

"Should we wake her up?"

Stella had been waiting for this. "You do it."

Darci shook her head. "She might get mad."

We stared at the envelope.

I put Stella's envelope and the rest of the mail on the kitchen counter. "Better safe than sorry, huh?"

Darci went back to cartoons. I went to Julio's.

Mom came home just after four. Julio and I were tossing a football back and forth on the street. Mom waved as she drove. I tossed the ball back to Julio. "I gotta go."

Julio held the ball under his arm. "When can we go for a ride in that jeep again?"

"Soon, I hope."

I jogged home.

Mom was getting her purse out of the car. She smiled. "What's going on, little big man?"

"Not much."

"Staying out of trouble, I hope."

"Yeah."

I followed Mom into the kitchen. She dropped her keys and purse onto the counter, frowning at the bills. She moved the junk mail aside . . . and froze.

She grabbed the card under the catalog. "Look at this."

"It's from Texas."

"Stella!" Mom called. She gave me a look I couldn't figure out. Like she was mad at me, or something. "Stella!"

"I'm coming, hang on."

Mom held the card up and gave me a stabbing look. "Did you know about this?"

"Well . . . yeah."

"And you didn't *tell* her?"

"She was asleep."

Mom closed her eyes. What was she so hot about?

Stella came into the kitchen. Her hair was wrapped in a towel.

Mom held up the envelope.

Stella snapped it out of her hand and tore it open. "Finally!"

She pulled the card out. A twenty-dollar bill fluttered to the counter. Stella started reading, smiling like she'd just won a trip to Disneyland.

Her smile faded.

Mom saw it, too. "What does it say, Stella?"

Stella handed the card to Mom and left the kitchen.

Mom read it and looked up.
"What?"
Mom handed it to me.

Dear Stella,
   Another birthday! I hope you are well
and that you are minding Mrs. Coconut.
I can't believe you're another year older.
You are growing up so fast it makes me
feel ancient. How can I have a fifteen-
year-old daughter? Tell me. How? It's
enough to make me cry. Well, enough of
my whining. Here's some money. You can
probably use it.
   Happy birthday.
   Love, Twyla

She didn't even know how old her own
daughter was. I looked up. "Fifteen?"
Mom shook her head.
The twenty-dollar bill lay with the junk
mail on the counter.

24

Typhoon

The next day, Sunday, I was in the yard chasing toads out of the grass with a stick when Ledward came over. He was in a good mood.

He bent close and whispered, even though no one else was around. "Today we pop the secret plan. You ready?"

I flung the stick into the bushes. "What do I do?"

"Just be yourself."

A half hour later Ledward, Mom, Darci, and I were on our way to the Humane Society in Ledward's jeep. Ledward had invited Stella, too, but she said, "I don't like cats, I don't like dogs, I don't like rabbits, and I don't like seeing anything in a cage, so somebody tell me why I would want to go."

Man, she was snippy.

When we got to the Humane Society, Ledward parked and turned to me. "Show your mama, boy."

Mom put up her hand to stop me. "Listen, we're just looking, right? Nobody's getting a dog." She looked straight into my eyes. "Are we clear about this?"

"Yeah, but—"

Mom put her finger on my lips. "Just. Looking."

There were people everywhere. Almost

every dog was barking. It was deafening. I covered my ears and pushed my way through.

"Streak! Stre—"

I gaped at Streak's empty kennel as my world crumbled. "But . . ."

Ledward, Mom, and Darci crowded around me. Ledward looked in the kennels on either side. No Streak. "Maybe somebody's got her out in the yard."

"No. They can't. She's mine!"

Mom put her hand on my shoulder. "Calvin, if someone wants to adopt her, that's a good thing, right? She'll have a home. Isn't that what you wanted for her?"

My head felt as if it was about to explode.

"You're back," someone said.

I whipped around. It was Ben, the guy we'd talked to before. A small wiener dog was tucked under his arm. Ben held it up. "Meet Olivine. She just came in."

I was frantic. "Where's Streak?"

"Who?"

"Streak . . . the dog I . . . the dog . . ."

I choked. It was all slipping away.

"Ohhh, you mean Ruby."

"That's the one," Ledward said.

Ben shook his head. "A lady just adopted her." He glanced back through the crowd. "Maybe she's still here. I don't know."

There was a big stir over by the offices. The crowd surged, people scrambling to see what

was going on. Someone shouted, "Come back! Here, doggie, doggie, doggie, here, doggie!"

"Loose dog." Ben set Olivine the wiener dog in Streak's vacant kennel and hurried off.

Who cared?

I hooked my fingers in the chain-link fence. The wiener dog looked up at me. She had long ears and a pointy nose. She was trembling.

Ledward tapped my shoulder. "Look."

I shook him off.

"Look."

25

A Dog-Size Flea

Ledward lifted his chin toward the dog everyone was trying to catch. It was black and white,
and fast.

"Streak!"

I promise, that crazy dog was laughing. She
was having a party. Nobody could touch her.

"Streak!" I shouted again.

Streak heard me. She tried to stop. Her paws slid on the concrete and she barreled into a wall.

I started running.

In an instant she was leaping at my feet, a dog-size flea. I picked her up and hugged her. Streak licked my face.

The crowd cheered, everyone laughing and clapping.

Mom's mouth hung open. Not one person could catch that dog and there she was licking my face.

"Ho!" Ben said, running up. "How'd you *do* that?"

A lady stumbled up behind him, gasping. "Oh, thank you, thank you!" She gulped, catching her breath. "Ruby, you naughty dog."

I turned so the lady couldn't touch her. "Her name is Streak."

"Calvin," Mom said, gently.

"She's mine, Mom."

The lady blinked.

Mom moved closer. "I'm sorry. He doesn't mean that. He was just here a couple of days ago and played with this dog, that's all."

Mom pried Streak out of my arms. She stroked her once and handed her to the lady. Streak wiggled and whined. The lady struggled to hang on to her.

"Good heavens!"

The lady dumped Streak into Ben's arms. "I think this one might be a little too much for me to handle."

My spirits soared. "Uh . . . there's a nice wiener dog in that kennel over there." I turned and pointed. "It just came in."

"He's right," Ben said. "I'll show you."

The lady sighed and nodded. "Is it calmer?"

"Oh, yes. Her name is Olivine, and she's a sweetheart." Ben handed Streak to me and winked.

Streak tickled my face with her wet nose. Darci reached up and Streak licked her hand.

Mom blinked. "I don't believe any of this."

"Can I get her, Mom, can I? Look, she loves me."

Mom wagged her finger at Ledward. "You."

Ledward gave her his best innocent face. "Me?"

"You knew I wouldn't be able to resist, didn't you?"

Ledward opened his hands.

Mom broke into a grin. "Oh, all right, you boys win. I guess one dog won't hurt." Then she wagged her finger at me. "But you keep her outside and away from Stella."

"Thanks, Mom! Thanks! I'll take good care of her, I promise."

"I know you'll try, honey. But really, you're

going to have to keep that dog outside. Or in your room. Away from Stella."

"I know, she might be allergic."

Mom gave Ledward a shove. "You, on the other hand, are in deep, deep trouble."

Ledward looked at me and flicked his eyebrows.

26

'ukus

At school the next day I sat at my desk thinking about Streak. The night before, I'd moved
down to the lower bunk so she could sleep
curled up by my feet, just like Chewy used to.
I smiled. Then I frowned, remembering I'd
left Streak fenced in the backyard before heading to school. I hoped she wasn't too lonely.

Mr. Purdy walked by and tapped my desk, which meant get to work and stop daydreaming.

We were supposed to be wrapping up our paragraphs. Mr. Purdy was going to tape them on the wall for everyone to read.

Someone sneezed.

A pencil fell to the floor.

The clock ticked.

Mr. Purdy paced. "Two minutes. Wrap it up."

I glanced around the room. Rubin was writing furiously, head low to the table. Julio sat with his arms crossed, looking out the door. Maya was scowling at her paper. Willy was nodding slowly, as if he was listening to music in his head. Shayla sat with her hands clasped, smiling at me.

I turned away.

My paragraph was done. I guessed. Probably. I liked what I'd written. It got me a dog, right? It must be okay.

"Time's up!"

Out on the playground I sat with Julio, Rubin, Maya, and Willy on top of the jungle gym. No one said much. Writing took a lot out of you. We were beat.

Julio pointed his chin. "Check it out."

I turned to look.

Frankie Diamond was heading our way. Behind him, his idiot friends Bozo and Tito jeered from the shade of a giant monkeypod tree. "Watch out, Frankie. You go by them you might get 'ukus! Bwahahahahaha!"

Frankie kept on coming.

Willy whispered, "What's 'ukus?"

"Cooties," Maya said. "Head lice."

"We got head lice?" Rubin asked.

Julio scoffed. "Not me, but maybe you."

"Shhh, Frankie's coming."

Frankie Diamond stood at the bottom of the jungle gym. He looked up at me, his hands on his hips. "So, you got that dog, or what?"

"Yeah! I did!"

Frankie Diamond nodded. "Cool. It was a good one."

"The best ever."

"Maybe sometime I come your house and check it out."

"Uh . . . yeah, sure . . . anytime."

Frankie nodded, once. He watched Rubin scratch his head. "You got 'ukus, or what?"

"No," Rubin said.

Frankie studied him a moment, then headed back over to the fools under the monkeypod tree.

Julio whistled, low. "That was strange."

I nodded.

"So," Maya said. "Is your mom going to let you keep Streak?"

I grinned. "If I don't let her in the house."

But still, I was worried.

Stella hadn't been exactly thrilled, even when Mom promised her that Streak would never come in the house. Stella could still make a big stink and blow it all up. If she did, Streak would have to go.

Rubin kept scratching his head. "What do you do with the dog while you're in school?"

"Leave her in the backyard. It's fenced."

I couldn't wait to get home. Streak and I had places to go! Me and my dog, cruising the neighborhood. Yeah!

Rubin scratched and scratched. Did he really have 'ukus? Were they like fleas? Did they jump from one head to another?

"I got an idea!" I said to Julio, Willy, and Maya. "Let's take Rubin over by Frankie and Tito so he can scratch his 'ukus. I bet they run away."

"Or kill us," Julio said.

"No, we just pretend to go by . . . close."

Rubin frowned . . . then grinned. "I got a better idea. How's about all of us go over there scratching?"

"Watch um run," I said.

We climbed down and headed over. I don't know how we suddenly got so brave, but it was hilarious to watch Frankie, Bozo, and Tito scramble away from us. We didn't even have to say a word.

27

Fleabag

That night Ledward came over with a fat stinky fish head for Streak to gnaw on. Streak snapped it out of Ledward's hand and carried it out into the yard, where she plopped down and ripped into it.

Mom winced and headed back into the house. "That's disgusting."

Ledward followed her. "Fish heads are good. They got a lot of vitamins, especially the eye."

"Can we change the subject?"

I crept closer to Streak for a better look at the fish head. It was shiny silver. It had a big eye. "Watch out for bones," I whispered. Mom always said that when we ate fish.

Streak thumped her tail.

Ledward stood over us. "I brought fresh ahi."

Ahi is tuna, and when Ledward cooks it on the hibachi with lemon and butter, there's nothing better. Except teriyaki meat sticks. Nothing beats that.

"Did the head come from that fish, Ledward?"

"Yep. Go start the fire."

I went out on the patio and got the hibachi going. As I was poking at the coals with a stick, Streak showed up. Her breath smelled like a garbage dump.

"Ho, man, you stink!"

She licked her lips. I pulled her close. Streak and my dad's dog Chewy in Las Vegas would probably go head to head over food. They were both professional eaters. Dinner comes. Boom! It's gone.

Ledward came out with a stack of ahi steaks. Streak's ears shot forward when Ledward laid the steaks on the sizzling hibachi and painted them with melted butter.

Ledward chuckled. "Look the dog. Still hungry."

"You should bring your pig over sometime. Let him play with Streak."

Ledward nodded. "That would be interesting."

We watched the fire.

I glanced back when the screen door slid open.

Stella's eyes were pinned on Streak. When Streak didn't get up to go jump all over her, she came out and eased the door shut behind her. "Smells good."

Ledward painted more butter on the ahi. "Fresh from the ocean today."

Streak was locked on the hibachi like a shark on blood.

Stella looked at me and said, "I just wanted to say your dog isn't so bad. I mean, it doesn't make my eyes get puffy. If it stays outside."

Was this a trick?

Stella looked up at the sky. "Nice night."

I followed her gaze.

"It's just . . . well . . . it's just that you wanted it so badly," she added, still looking at the sky.

Huh?

"Anyway," Stella said. "Keep that fleabag out of my room."

She went back into the house.

I turned to Ledward.

He grunted. "She just told you the dog can stay."

"She did?"

"Long as you keep it out of the house."

We tapped fists. We did it!

Before I fell asleep that night, I heard Ledward roll the lawn mower out of the garage. It was pitch-black out. Streak was curled up on the bunk under me.

I turned over and looked out the window. I could see Ledward's shadow in the driveway, bending over the lawn mower.

He pulled the cord.

Errrrrrrrrrrrrrrrr!

It started! And stayed started.

Ledward let it run for thirty seconds or so and shut it down. "You hear that, boy?" he called through the screen.

"It works."

"Now you can mow the lawn and I can go home."

Ledward rolled the lawn mower back into the garage, came back out, and stood by my window. "That dog in there with you?"

"Yeah."

"Good night, then."

"Good night. Ledward?"

"Yeah?"

"I'll cut the grass."

Ledward chuckled, then started up his jeep. He gave the horn a short toot and drove off.

I listened as the sound of the engine got

smaller and smaller and all I could hear were the toads croaking down by the river.

And Streak.

Snoring on the bunk below me.

Hawaii Fact:

One of the wettest spots in the world is on the island of Kauai. Mount Waialeale consistently records rainfall of nearly five hundred inches per year.

Calvin Fact:

Every year around fourteen bugs crawl into your mouth while you're sleeping. And guess what? You swallow most of them. People study this stuff.

 **Graham Salisbury** is the author of two Calvin Coconut books: *Trouble Magnet* and *The Zippy Fix,* as well as several novels for older readers, including the award-winning *Lord of the Deep, Blue Skin of the Sea, Under the Blood-Red Sun, Eyes of the Emperor, House of the Red Fish,* and *Night of the Howling Dogs.* Graham Salisbury grew up in Hawaii. Calvin Coconut and his friends attend the same school Graham did—Kailua Elementary School. Graham now lives in Portland, Oregon, with his family. Visit him on the Web at www.grahamsalisbury.com.

 **Jacqueline Rogers** has illustrated more than ninety books for young readers over the past twenty years. She studied illustration at the Rhode Island School of Design. You can visit her at www.jacquelinerogers.com.